The Secret of the Ice Castle

&

Other Inspirational Tales

By Heidi M. Thomas

Illustrations by Susie Talbot

SunCatcher Publications

Advance Praise for Inspirational Fairytales

"This book reminded me of a combination of Bill Bennett's *Book of Virtues* and *Lord of the Rings*. Very relatable & applicable. For anyone who's been on life's journey, I think they'll find something of relevance in each story." – Brenda Cox Clayton, *Desperate Wives - Help and Hope for Women Considering Separation or Divorce* and *Sharing Your Faith Journey*

"*Inspirational Fairytales* will warm your heart. Heidi M. Thomas's magical stories fire the imagination with hope and faith. Gentle lessons free the mind to accept the super-natural along with the realities of taking responsibility, experiencing the joy of sharing, and turning to God in both joy and sorrow." – Mary E. Trimble, *Maureen*

I loved these *Inspirational Fairytales*. They were just what I needed. I completely related to the story in the Afterword—being offered help but continuing to hold onto the burden and carry it myself. Now, since reading the Fairytales, I keep thinking of the passage quoted at the beginning, Matthew 11:28: "Come to me...I will give you rest." The stories were really interesting and well-written. They were light and easy. They lightened my heart, and clearly demonstrated the theme. Thank you for writing them. Nicely done. – Milana Marsenich, *Copper Sky* and *The Swan Keeper.*

"These stories convey powerful messages about burdens we carry alone when we do not have to do so. They are short enough to not be too overpowering to small children in 1st through 5th grade, but could have been written even for an adult perspective.

Thomas has written stories concerning man's selfishness and turning away from pursuing our heavenly father as our earthly problems only grow larger and larger and not turning to the Father to take our burdens. The stories tell the struggles between being concerned of this earth and not concerned with spiritual needs. – Barbara Jaquay, *Where Have All the Sheep Gone? Sheep Herders and Ranchers in Arizona - A Disappearing Industry*

"This collection of Christian fantasy short stories based on the theme of Matthew 11:28 encourages us to overcome the problems we face in life. The stories are entertaining and would be perfect for a fun family read aloud and discussion time." – Natalie Bright, *Keep 'em Full and Keep 'em Rollin'*

A SunCatcher Publications book

Cover Design by Jason McIntyre
www.TheFarthestReaches.com

Cover Illustration by Susie Talbot

Secret of the Ice Castle photo courtesy Pixabay

Library of Congress Cataloguing-in-Publication data is available on file.

ISBN - 978-0-9990663-2-4

Printed in the United States of America

10 9 8 7 6 5 4 3 2 1

"Come to me, all you who are tired and carrying heavy loads. I will give you rest."
Matthew 11:28

THE SECRET OF THE ICE CASTLE

Once upon a time in a shiny white castle, with walls made of ice, Princess Bianca was born. From an early age, she knew exactly what to do to be a good girl. Dressed all in white, and her red hair long and shining, she was neat and tidy. She minded her parents, King Ulrich and Queen Millicent. She knew just what to say. She entertained them and made them laugh.

"Look at our perfect little Princess." Her mother and father smiled with pride.

Bianca grew up within the white, icy walls of the castle. She wandered the long halls and hummed her way through her days. She learned to read and studied all the books in the library—history and literature, music and manners, and rules of religion. She ate formal dinners with the King and Queen, who also dressed completely in white.

Her parents never took her out of the ice castle into the Kingdom. The seasons came and went, but everything inside remained the same. The castle was all she knew. She seldom had anyone to play with other than her family or the servants, so whenever visitors came, the shy princess hid, peeking out from around the corner. When she met one of the King and Queen's subjects, she stood quietly with eyes downcast, never speaking.

The visitors dressed differently—in browns and greens and blues—they spoke of other kingdoms and told tales of magical forests, endless seas and cool breezes. As Princess Bianca grew older, she became curious about the world outside the castle, because the visitors would often bring tree branches full of green luscious leaves and beautiful, happy flowers that splashed reds, yellows, and pinks against the white walls.

One day her curiosity got the best of her. "When may I go out into the Kingdom? I'm ten years old now."

The Queen drew in a sharp breath and put a protective arm around Bianca's shoulder. "Oh no, you mustn't! You must stay here with us."

Bianca widened her eyes, wondering why, but she was an obedient daughter, so she did not ask again.

Time went on. She grew taller and celebrated several more birthdays. The Princess learned how to do fine needlepoint. She played the harp and sang every day. Her thoughts kept returning to the visitors and where they might live. She yearned to see the places that grew such colorful flowers. *This castle is a wonderful, perfect place, but what is it like outside?*

One day, somewhat bored with her perfect life, she explored the library, looking for answers. As she gazed at the tall shelves of brown leather books, she was drawn to a thick, black book, called The Bible. She took it from the shelf and began to read about an all-knowing, loving God who had created the earth, the seas and the heavens, the animals and birds, and a wonderful, beautiful garden called Eden. *Is this the world of colors and other kingdoms and people, like the visitors tell about?* It sure sounded like it. She thought about what she read. *What would it be like to find this world, so different from the Ice Castle?*

Princess Bianca asked her parents about this God and His world, but they were too busy running the Kingdom to give her any answers. A yearning grew inside her heart. *I want to know more about the world outside. I wonder where I could find this God who made it.*

One day, her father and mother called her into their snowy white chambers. The King stood, his face as if carved in stone. "The time has come for us to allow you to go out into the Kingdom and learn about the world."

Bianca's heart danced with happiness, and she gave her parents a huge smile.

"But," Queen Millicent's dark brows drew low on her forehead, "you mustn't forget your family and what we have taught you, and you must know that no one outside this castle can be trusted."

Bianca frowned. From what she had observed when the visitors came, it did seem that her mother and father didn't trust anyone.

Her mother took from her pocket a small heart-shaped locket on a gold chain and placed it around Bianca's neck. The cold metal made the Princess shiver. She fingered the smooth gold.

"This will be your guide." The Queen peered into Bianca's eyes. "It is to remind you that our thoughts will always be with you and will protect you. You must never open this locket. It holds the secret of the castle. And, you must remember to *never* reveal this secret to anyone."

Bianca forgot her perfect manners and clapped and bounced from one foot to the other. "Hooray! I'm going out into the Kingdom! Thank you, thank you!"

At her parents' somber expressions, she stopped. She rubbed her forehead and squished her eyebrows together, for she did not know what the secret of the castle was. But she was afraid to ask, because it seemed like the King and Queen expected her to know. She didn't want to disappoint them. And if she questioned them, they might change their minds and not let her leave.

So the next morning, Princess Bianca set off on her journey into the Kingdom. She stared in awe at the beautiful forest that surrounded the Ice Castle—the giant trees, the lush ferns, the soft moss. Everything was brilliant green, and the sun smiled on her with its warm amber light. The trees seemed to beckon to her. "Come and talk to us," they whispered.

Bianca ran into the forest, laughing and skipping. "Hello, great and mighty trees. I am the Princess. I come from the Ice Castle, where I live with my mother and father, the Queen and King of this land."

Just then she thought she felt the locket and gold chain tug at her neck. Oh, was she not supposed to tell that? Was that the secret?

Princess Bianca slowed her steps as she continued down the path. Everyone knew the King and Queen, and that they lived in the Ice Castle. That couldn't be the secret. She went back to skipping.

The wind sang in the trees, a lovely melody that soothed Bianca's thoughts. She smiled at an olive-colored frog that hopped across her path and waved at a bluebird who sat on a branch of an evergreen tree. It was truly a beautiful world this God had created.

Then she heard a deep voice off to the side of the path. "Hello, Princess." A great brown bear let out a low growl. "What a pretty locket you're wearing."

Bianca stopped. Trembling tingles rushed from her toes all the way up into her head. "H-Hello." How did the bear know she was a princess?

"I know everything that goes on in my forest." The bear spoke as if she could hear the Princess's thoughts. "I know you are from the Ice Castle, and I know your mother and father are the Queen and King. I won't hurt you. Why don't you come with me and meet my children?" She pointed toward a sunny meadow where two soft, fuzzy bear cubs ran and leapt and giggled.

They're so cute! "Oh, that would be great fun." But as Bianca took a step off the path, the necklace tugged at her neck. The words of her mother came back to her. "You must never trust anyone…" Were these bears dangerous? Did they want the secret? A chill raced up her back. No, she mustn't interact with them.

She stepped back onto the path. "Maybe another day, thank you." She gave a slight bow. Princess Bianca continued her walk, peering into the woods around her, and flinching at any noise. She didn't want to run into another animal and risk the secret of the castle.

After what seemed like hours, she came to the edge of the woods and saw a small village nestled in a valley. Children in colorful clothing played near the path, with joined hands, and sang a rhyme as they danced in a circle.

That looks like fun. With a smile, she stopped to watch, her toes tapping. When the children saw her, they stopped dancing and singing. They stood still and stared at Bianca.

Why did they stare? Maybe she looked very tall to them, and perhaps her white dress and red hair was unusual in this village.

"Hello. My name is Bianca. May I join in your game?"

But the children stood, staring at her, not saying a word. After what seemed a long time, one of the bigger boys stepped forward.

"You are different from us." He scrunched his face in a frown. "We do not like you." With a snort, he turned, and all the children ran away.

A cloud passed over the sun. The Princess stood as if rooted to the spot. A hot tear trickled from her eye, and her heart sat heavy in her chest. She drew herself up to her full height, took a deep breath and said out loud, "I don't care. They just don't know me. Besides, they are not to be trusted."

The locket hung heavy as she turned away and walked slowly back to the Ice Castle. She walked with her head bowed, the chain tugging at her neck. It must be her imagination, but the locket seemed larger to her now.

Toward evening she reached her home, and the brilliant white light of the Ice Castle welcomed her. At least here, she was liked. The King and Queen smiled and patted her shoulder.

"We're so glad you're back safe and sound. You did very well today. You remembered that no one is to be trusted, and you did not tell the secret of the castle." The Queen reached out and touched the necklace, smiling at her daughter.

Again, Bianca wondered what the secret was, but she was so confused about what she had seen and so sad and tired from her journey that she soon fell asleep and forgot to ask.

+++

Despite her curiosity and questions, Bianca stayed close to home, for every time she ventured out into the kingdom, the necklace grew heavier. She stood up straighter and taller to carry the weight without stumbling. The small gold locket had grown to the size of an apple.

The question continued to live inside her mind. What kind of a secret could it be? Was it something very terrible? Had someone in her family done something bad?

Maybe she was adopted. She was red-haired and had green eyes, and everyone else in her family had dark hair and dark eyes. Maybe she wasn't really a princess. But she could never ask her parents. They would be so disappointed in her. And more than anything, she did not want to make them unhappy. They thought she was the perfect Princess, that she always did everything just right and pleased them. Maybe she could peek inside the locket. But then the heaviness on her neck stopped her. She had been told never to open it.

The questions churned through her mind. Bianca no longer hummed her way through the days, barely ate her meals, and at night she could hardly sleep. She stared at the necklace, imploring it to give her answers. But it simply hung there, becoming duller and heavier.

+++

Several years passed. Princess Bianca kept reading the stories in the Bible and wondering about the world. She was no longer satisfied to live in the confining castle walls, behaving herself perfectly. She sighed. *I can't live like this anymore. Maybe God will know.* The book said He was all-knowing. *But where is He?* She hadn't found Him within the icy castle or on her short journeys beyond. That meant she needed to go farther out into the Kingdom to find Him…and maybe the answers to her questions.

One morning Bianca crawled out of her bed, yawning, and rubbing her eyes. *I'm so tired. Tired of wondering, tired of living without answers.* She squared her shoulders and strode to the royal chamber. Her heart pounded. Would they allow her to go out? And if they did, would she find what she was looking for?

As her parents lounged over breakfast, she told them she must leave and go out into the world on her own.

Her mother wept. "Oh, my little girl is all grown up and leaving me." She reached out and gently touched the golden locket. "Keep this with you always. It will remind you of us."

The King said, "Just remember what we have taught you. Be careful."

The Princess left the castle, her legs shaky and her whole body trembling. She didn't want to leave her mother and father. They were the only ones she had ever known or trusted. She didn't know how she could talk to other people, because in the past they had shunned her and made fun of her. Her breaths became short. What would she discover out in the kingdom and beyond? Dizzy, she gulped in a lungful of sweet air, held it, and then let it out slowly. *I must learn the secret on my own.* She trudged on.

Finally, she came to the village where a long time ago the children had run away from her. Bianca stopped by the well to get a cool drink of water. A handsome young man, wearing a wolf pelt over his shoulders, stopped. He proudly showed her the stag he had killed.

"Do you know the secret of the castle and where God lives?" she asked.

The hunter looked up and down at her red hair and flowing white dress and smiled. His perfect white teeth flashed. "Come with me, and I will show you."

Bianca's shoulders relaxed. Someone from the village actually talked to her! Maybe he would have the answers. She turned and walked down a path into the woods with him. The hunter bragged about all the game he hunted and how strong he was. They walked farther and farther into the dark woods.

"Is this where God lives?" she asked after a long time.

He stopped, reached out to touch her hair, and looked deep into her eyes. "What an unusual locket. What's in it?"

She felt it hang heavy on her neck. A coal-black crow cawed in a tree nearby. She shivered. Her mother's voice echoed in her mind: *Trust no one.*

"Oh, nothing. Where are we going?"

"It's just a little farther." The hunter's white teeth flashed in the dimness, like a wolf's. "Come on."

Bianca shivered. "No, thank you. I must go back." She turned and ran back toward the village as though her feet were on fire.

Shaking and breathless, she came upon an old woman dressed in a cloak of many colors—reds, blues, greens, and yellows—spinning bright red yarn. The woman looked at her and kept on spinning.

"Excuse me." Bianca swallowed hard. "I'm thirsty. May I have a drink?"

The old woman nodded toward a water bucket. "Who are you and what are you doing here?"

Princess Bianca drank the cool, sweet water and gave her name. "I'm looking for answers. Do you know the secret of the castle?" she blurted, "and why am I different from everyone else?"

The old woman never stopped spinning. "Ask and it will be given to you. Seek and you will find. Knock, and the door will be opened to you."

Bianca's brow knotted. "Ask who—?"

The spinner spoke again in those mysterious tones. "You must go find the Wise Man of the Mountain."

"But where—?" Bianca tried again, but the woman bent over her spinning wheel and hummed to herself.

The Princess turned away from the old woman. The gold necklace felt heavier than ever. She held it in one hand to relieve the pressure on her neck. Now she had more questions than before. She played with the latch, but did not dare open it.

On she went, asking everyone she met, "What is the secret? Where do I find the Mountain? Is that where God is?" But no one gave her any answers.

+++

Princess Bianca walked and walked. She came to another village and then another. No one would tell her the secret. Some people tried to trick her to find out what was in her locket. They told her stories, such as "God is the Universe," and "God is everyone. *You* are God." Or even, "There is no God." She cried out to the night sky, to the trees, and to the rocks. There was no answer. No one could help her. She sank to her knees, weariness heavy on her shoulders, and she finally slept.

One day she came to a clearing in the forest. Shimmering and glowing in the green meadow was a small house-size castle made of gold. The Princess stopped and stared in wonder. What could this be? Was this what she was looking for? Surely she would find answers in such a magical place.

Bianca walked toward the open door and peered inside. Everything was covered in gold. This must be the right place. Surely she would find answers here. She followed a gold brocade carpet up the hall to a large room with a high, domed ceiling. In the center on a sparkling jeweled throne sat a white-bearded man in golden robes.

"Welcome, my child." His voice was like deep, stringed music. "You have come to the right place. Please sit down and rest."

"Oh, thank you." Bianca was dizzy with exhaustion. Had she finally found God? "I have been walking for such a long time, and searching and wondering, and I am so confused and so tired. Can you help me? Do you know what the secret of the Ice Castle is?"

The old man smiled. "I know many secrets. But first you must give up something of value."

The Princess felt her eyes grow round as saucers. "My father and mother are the King and Queen, and they have many riches, but I have brought nothing with me."

"Then you must stay here with me and be my servant, until you know what you are looking for," the old man replied.

So for many days Bianca brought him food and drink, stood nearby and fanned him when he was warm. She brought him fruit when he was hungry and picked flowers for his table. Every day she asked him to give her the secret or to tell her where to find the mountain where God lived, but he just sent her off to clean his chambers or fetch more wine.

Bianca thought she should leave and continue her search. Or maybe she should just go home. But this was such a beautiful castle, in such a beautiful place. It certainly would be easier to stay here than to continue her tiring, frustrating journey. Questions and sadness burdened her heart.

One day, when she asked her question, the old man looked at her for a long time. "That necklace appears to be very valuable. I would be glad to accept it as a gift to the gods of secrets, and then maybe you will find what you have been looking for."

Suddenly the necklace jerked her head forward, almost throwing her to her knees. It seemed that her mother's voice spoke directly into her ear. "Remember what we have taught you."

The Princess stood up straight and tall. "No. This is a keepsake from my mother and father. I will not give it up." She turned and walked out of the gold castle and back toward the woods. As she turned and looked back, a cloud settled over the castle and its brilliant glow dimmed.

That was not the God I read about. That man had no answers. The necklace felt larger and heavier than ever. But she must protect it, so she carried it in her arms as she continued on her journey.

Bianca missed the King and Queen and the safety of the Ice Castle. She was afraid to meet anyone else because she could trust no one. But the question of the secret burned within her, and she had to find the answer. The only one who knew must be God, but first she must find the mountain.

She traveled many miles, cradling the large locket with both arms because its weight on the chain pulled on her neck. Her shoulders ached. She slept under trees, ate berries, and drank from the many streams she crossed. She wandered through valleys and climbed over hills, asking the questions over and over. She no longer noticed the beauty of the Kingdom around her. Bianca's eyes burned, her body moved sluggishly, and her heart felt like it had shrunk. Maybe she should go home again where everything was wonderful, everyone loved her, and life was easy. But that would be admitting failure. Her mother and father would be so disappointed in her. Maybe she could go back to the village. Maybe they would accept her now that she was a grown-up.

"No, I can't go back. I must do this on my own." She spoke aloud, trying to find the will and the courage to go on.

Then one afternoon she came to the foot of a tall mountain. She gazed up and up at the top, which was covered in clouds, and she slumped to the ground.

"I am so tired. This necklace is so heavy. I cannot climb up there. I will never find God who can give me the answer." She sobbed for a long time, rocking the necklace like a baby, until night came. Finally she fell into a deep sleep.

In her dream the breeze whispered to her, "Seek God's kingdom. Then the answers will be given to you."

"But where...?" She'd already been walking for such a long time.

"You must climb."

"No, I can't. I am too tired; I can't go on. I'll never find the secret. I give up." Despair settled around her like a dark cloud.

"You *can* do it," the breeze murmured. "You *must* do it."

+++

Bianca awoke in the morning, refreshed. She looked up to the top of the mountain, with its peak hidden in the clouds. "I *must* climb."

So the Princess set off, carrying the heavy locket. She set one foot in front of the other and slowly pulled herself over the jagged gray rocks up the steep mountainside. The tree line above loomed dense and dark.

Then a strong gust of wind swirled dirt into Bianca's eyes and raindrops pelted her. Thunder exploded and lightning pierced the sky. She grasped a large rock and hung on as the wind and rain lashed at her. Her fingers bled, blowing branches scratched her face, and the temperature turned icy. *I'm going to be blown off this mountain.* "Help me," she shrieked into the tempest.

Darkness descended, and she clung to the boulder, her fingers frozen into claws around it. She shivered so violently she thought she would dislodge the rock. Why had she come up here? This was such foolishness, that she thought she could find the Secret on her own. "Oh, Mummy, Papa," she reverted to names she hadn't used since she was about four, "I've failed you. I'm so sorry." She sobbed, her tears mingling with the rain. *I'm going to die.* Her fingers gave way and she slipped from the stone.

+++

Gradually, Bianca became aware of birdsong and her face felt warm instead of icy. She opened her eyes a slit to take in a crystal blue sky. *Am I dead?* She lifted her head and widened her eyes. Above, etched against the sky, soared a bright snowy peak. Nestled under the boulder's overhang, Bianca flexed her fingers and toes and stretched her arms and legs. No, she wasn't dead—she was still half way up this steep mountain. *I'm going to turn back home.*

She looked over her shoulder only to see a sharp drop-off below. She gulped. *How did I get up here, and how did I not get blown into that precipice?* There didn't seem to be any way to get down again. A hot tear trickled from her eye. *I'm trapped.*

The soft breeze wafted over her, calling softly. "You may weep for a night, but joy comes in the morning. Climb upward. You can do it."

"I've come this far. I have to continue." Bianca rose, took a deep breath and set out once again. It seemed to take forever to climb, but the breeze blew behind her, encouraging her, whispering to her, "You can do it. You can do it."

Finally, when she could barely take another step, she came to a velvety, emerald-green meadow. A large clear-blue lake, rimmed with soft green trees, shimmered in the sunlight. Weary beyond words, Bianca sank to her knees by the water.

"Hello. Is anyone here?" she called, but no one answered. "What is the Secret? Where is God? Who *am* I?" Her tears flowed into the lake.

Then she heard a soft voice in the lapping of the waves, through the rustle of the trees. "Give me your burden, and you will know."

Bianca wrinkled her brow. "My burden?"

"You are tired and carrying a heavy load. Come to me. I will give you rest," the voice replied.

The necklace tugged at her neck. She looked down at the heart-shaped locket. It certainly was heavy, all right.

"That can't be it. I can't take it off. I was entrusted to take care of it. This is my link to my family, my protection from the world."

The necklace grew larger. Her arms were weak and shaky from holding it. "But I can't go on carrying this heavy thing. I'm not strong enough." Tears came to her eyes. "I do need help. Oh, God, is that you? Can you give me the answer?"

Slowly she lifted the locket in her hands and held it for a long time, gazing into the dull gold surface. "What is the secret? Why won't you tell me?"

With beating heart and trembling fingers, she pried open the latch. What would she find? Was the secret really inside? She struggled with the catch until the lid flew open. A moth flew out. She gazed open-mouthed.

It was empty.

She gasped. Her hands covered her face. What had she done? Had she betrayed the secret? Had she destroyed the bond to her family?

"There never was a secret, only fear and distrust that has burdened your heart." The voice soothed from the lapping waves. "You don't need to carry the burdens of your family. You have been pushed hard from all sides, but you need not be beaten down. Don't lose hope. I am with you always."

"There is *no secret*?" She turned toward the forest, then back to the lake, her mouth opening and closing, tears forming hot in her eyes. "That can't be true." Had the Queen lied to her? She fell to her knees, weeping until no more tears came.

"Your parents are good people," said the quiet, compassionate voice. "They were only trying to protect you from hurt and heartache. They love you. And so do I."

"No! No one loves me." Bianca turned from the lake, following a stream into the forest. "How could they let me carry this heaviness for so long without telling me?" She ran, sobbing, until she couldn't continue. Once again, she fell to the ground and buried her face in her hands. Her heart was as empty as the locket. Sorrow weighed heavily on her shoulders. At last, sleep overcame her.

When she awoke, she became aware of water trickling, gurgling, rippling. Bianca followed the sound to a waterfall splashing merrily from a high boulder. She looked down at her dirty clothing, felt her disheveled hair. Hesitantly, she waded into the stream and under the waterfall. She stood, allowing the water to cascade over her, tinkling, laughing, singing. As she listened to the music of the waterfall, her sorrowful, heavy doubts and fears seemed to wash away into the stream.

Bianca finally got out, feeling cleansed and purified. She walked slowly back to the lake, where she found a patch of ripe, red strawberries. Refreshed, she sat in the cool shade of a mountain oak tree.

The gentle voice spoke again. "You can trust me. I love you, and I will always be with you. You'll never be alone again. You have been set free."

A chorus of birds trilled, the waves soothed the shore, and the warmth of the sun eased her hunched shoulders. She couldn't understand it, but a feeling of peace enveloped her as if the voice's presence had melted the icy grip of fear. Bianca looked up into the sky. "Oh, I do, I do trust you."

And for the first time since she could remember, she suddenly felt a lightness about her and realized she barely felt the small locket around her neck. Her burden had flown away like the moth. She stood and opened her arms to the soft greens and blues of the lake and the forest and the sky. Spinning and dipping, she danced and sang until she fell, dizzy, into a soft rainbow bed of wildflowers. The Princess breathed in their perfume and felt the velvety petals as they covered her white dress with yellow, blue, pink and purple. She laughed out loud.

Bianca realized she had talked with God, and that He would be with her always. She need never be afraid again. She was strong, ready for something new, to make her own way, her own life. But first she would go home and share what she'd learned in the Bible and on this journey with her parents.

No more fear. No more distrust—only the Truth. She was free.

THE FIRETENDER

Thalia awoke early. Birds chirped and wind rustled in the trees. She snuggled into the fur covers on her soft, dry mattress of leaves and pine needles. But she couldn't lie still for long.

This was a Day of Celebration for her, a special event in her clan, to mark passage into womanhood. It was a time for feasting and gift giving. Most exciting of all was the special gift she would receive from someone important in her family, Aunt Vesta.* Her aunt had been hinting about it and teasing her for weeks, and Thalia could hardly wait to find out what the gift would be. Aunt Vesta was an important woman in the clan, and the gift would most likely be extra special.

She slipped out of her bed and outside the animal skin yurt, stretched slowly, gazing at the brilliant blue of the sky and the golden glow of the sunrise. No one else was up yet. Her mind buzzed. She would be the "Woman of Honor"—the day was all hers. She skipped into the woods, humming and picking flowers and dreaming about the presents she would receive.

Then she heard voices of the other children calling her. "Thalia, come play!"

Dancing, singing and games, eating, and much laughter filled the day. Thalia's joy spread to all those around her. Her laughter was like music as she swung her long dark hair in the celebration dances. The other children flocked to her as she teased them gently, and the adults laughed at her jokes. The "Clan of the Fire People" was like one large family. Thalia had many mothers and fathers, aunts and uncles, brothers and sisters, and she loved them all. But she was closest of all to Aunt Vesta. Some day she would be an important woman in the clan, like her aunt.

At the end of the day, the clan gathered in a circle around Thalia. The drums throbbed, and the children sang clear, sweet notes. Thalia's heart did a little dance in her chest and her toes wiggled impatiently in her moccasins. At last Aunt Vesta stepped forward.

"This is Thalia," she said solemnly. "Today is her Day of Celebration, and it is the beginning of a journey—a step out of childhood onto the path to adulthood."

The clan cheered and clapped. The drumbeat swelled. Vesta smiled. "And now to help Thalia along her way, let us present her with our gifts."

The youngest child stepped forward, shyly holding out a collection of smooth shiny stones. The next one offered Thalia a beaded bracelet she had made herself. Inside the circle, Thalia received carrying bags made from soft skins; she squealed in delight over a bearskin rug for her yurt, and delighted in pictures painted in vivid colors from the juices of berries and plants. One by one, from the youngest to the oldest, each member of her clan presented her with a special gift. The pile grew with beads, shells, quillwork, arrowheads, furs, and skins.

The last to come forward was Aunt Vesta, to give her the most precious offering. "Now, I want to present this special girl with an important gift. I am old. I have served you all for many years, and I must leave soon on my final journey. It is time that my responsibilities pass on to a young person." Aunt Vesta's voice was deep and serious. "I have chosen you, Thalia, to follow in my footsteps, to keep safe the one treasure we hold dearest—Fire. The gods have been good to me and to our people by giving us this gift."

Thalia's stomach did a giant flip-flop as her aunt came toward her. Vesta's gnarled, leathery brown hands held a brick-red clay pot filled with live coals.

"This is your gift from me. I am entrusting the Spirit of Fire to you. It is now your responsibility to keep it alive for the clan and for all the children yet to come. You must feed Fire every day to keep it alive. The Spirit of Fire will become you, and you will become the Spirit."

Thalia swallowed hard. The sounds of laughter and music faded around her as she stretched her hands out to take the gift. This was the greatest honor that could be given to her. She had been watching her aunt tend Fire ever since she could remember. Now Thalia must take great care of Fire and make her favorite aunt proud. Most of all, she must keep Fire safe for the clan's survival and prestige.

For the rest of the evening she kept the container close by, glancing at it every few minutes, as she watched the others dancing. She didn't want to let it out of her sight, so when the other children asked her to join them, she just smiled and shook her head, patting the container by her side.

Where shall I keep Fire? She tried to remember what Aunt Vesta had done and what her instructions were. She knew she must keep it close by always and make sure nothing happened to its spirit, for hers was the only Clan to possess Fire.

Later, when she prepared for bed, she had an idea. "That's it! I shall keep it in bed with me!" But as she started to cover Fire's container with her bed covers, Aunt Vesta's head peeked through the door.

"No! No! It must not be covered. It must have some air to stay alive. Let me show you how to bank it properly."

By now Thalia was so terrified Fire would die that she could not sleep. She got up often to peek into the container, making sure the warm glow of the coals was still there. By morning she felt heavy with tiredness. She lay her head down on her bed—just for a moment.

"Get up, my dear," boomed Aunt Vesta's voice from the doorway. "You have responsibilities now."

Thalia sat upright. "Oh no, have I let it go out?" Tears stung her eyes as she reached for the Fire container. *Maybe I'm not able to do this!*

"No, dear, there are still live coals. You must get Fire going for the women to cook, and you must watch and feed it all day to make sure it does not die down. Let me show you how to start the flames fresh each morning."

Her aunt then taught Thalia how to blow gently on the warm coals, to feed their glow with dried leaves and bits of twigs. "The Fire god sent me this gift with a swift, jagged fire spear from the sky, and I have been keeping it safe ever since. If it dies, no one knows how to get it again. Fire is my greatest pride and joy."

Thalia breathed deep. *Yes, I can do this. I will make Aunt Vesta proud.*

The days continued, as her aunt taught Thalia and watched her as she learned to tend Fire.

Finally, to Thalia's great sadness, the day came when Aunt Vesta departed on her final journey. But Thalia was too busy to mourn her aunt for long. All day she fed Fire twigs and branches she gathered and fanned it for the women of the clan. By night she could barely keep her eyes open. She banked Fire carefully as Aunt Vesta had shown her, put the glowing coals into the special clay container, and sank into a deep sleep. In her dreams Fire chased her, then it turned and ran away, leaving her shivering and frightened.

Her eyes flew open in the darkness. *Where is it? Did I let it die?* She grabbed the container. As her eyes rested on the coals' comforting glow, she breathed deeply. Fire was still alive.

The next day, after she had Fire blazing for the women, Thalia sat and watched a group of children play her favorite game. They laughed and shouted as they chased each other around.

"Come on, Thalia," one of them cried. Forgetting her responsibility with Fire, she jumped up and joined the other children. She ran, she leaped, she shouted, and she laughed. Her long black hair flew around her face, and her bare feet danced and whirled, her face alight with a great joy.

"Thalia! Come quickly! Fire is dying!" One of the women stood in the clearing, hands on her hips. Thalia looked back with a start. Fire. Oh, no, she had forgotten all about it while having fun. She mustn't do that again. She couldn't fail Aunt Vesta and the Clan's trust in her. With a sad smile, she looked back at the children and returned to her duties.

Thalia tended to Fire, feeding it during the day and banking it carefully at night.

"You are such a good Firetender," said the women of the clan. "We are so lucky to have such a responsible girl to take over Vesta's duties." Thalia stood a little taller when they told her that, and she smiled solemnly. A warmth glowed inside as she cared for Fire; she felt a kinship with it, as though feeding it also fed herself. She could be proud—she was living up to Aunt Vesta's expectations.

But Fire kept Thalia very, very busy. It was always hungry and forever demanding attention. She constantly gathered wood to feed it. She no longer had time for the beautiful bead necklaces she loved to create. Hers always had the brightest beads, with the most intricate designs, and neighboring clans wanted to trade for them. Thalia kept thinking about how happy she had been while making the lovely jewelry.

One evening, after she had banked Fire carefully and put it in her sleeping quarters, she crept back outside into the bright moonlight to work with her beads. Soon she forgot how tired she was from the hard work of tending Fire, and she hummed to herself.

A twig snapped close by. The beads spilled from her lap as she leaped up. She peered into the darkness. Then she saw him—a young man from a neighboring clan that had no Fire. He held her container of coals.

"Stop!" Thalia dashed toward him.

The young man jumped as he saw her, dropped the clay pot in his haste and ran into the night.

"My Fire." Thalia sobbed. "He came to steal my Fire. I can *never* leave it for such frivolous activities again."

And so Thalia continued on, working harder, never letting her attention wander. She became the best Firetender ever. The word spread among the clans, and many came with skins and jewels and exotic berries, wanting to trade for a coal of Fire. But the Clan voted to keep Fire for themselves. That way they would be the most powerful in the world.

"Aunt Vesta would be so proud of you," they told her. She smiled solemnly. Her head bowed, because she missed playing games with her friends, doing her beadwork, and wandering in the woods all day. She'd had no worries then. She was certain there would always be food, shelter, and a warm bed when she came home.

When she caught herself thinking these thoughts, she sat up straighter and scolded herself for letting her mind wander. She had an important responsibility, and she mustn't let herself stray from her purpose. She busied herself gathering more wood and twigs and fanned the flames all day. At night she banked the coals carefully, guarding them with her very being.

But as time passed, it became harder and harder to keep the blaze going the way the Clan wanted it. Instead of saying, "You're the best Firetender ever," they would shout, "More wood! We need a hotter Fire! Can't you build it bigger?"

Thalia tried to please them all. She ran farther into the woods, gathered more fuel, and fanned the flames harder. But Fire just seemed to grow smaller. It no longer leaped and danced, its bright flames crackling and spinning in the wind.

"What am I doing wrong?" She ran faster, piled on more wood, and fanned desperately. Her tears flowed and dampened the flames. "Oh, Aunt Vesta, I am failing you," she sobbed.

The women of the Clan looked at the dying Fire in disgust and turned away with sneers. "If you can't do the simple job of tending Fire, then what good are you?"

Thalia cried and cried. Her tears rained on Fire until the flames were completely gone. She sat for a long time in the darkness, shivering in the cold. Her heart was empty. Her Fire dead. She had disgraced the clan, lost their Fire and their favored status in the world. She had failed.

As the chill wind crept into her bones, Thalia at last gathered the dark dead coals into the clay pot, wrapped it in a carrying bundle and walked alone into the woods. She kept walking throughout the night. When morning came, she found herself at the edge of a clearing where another clan lived. *Maybe I can get something to eat here.*

A group of women eating cold grains and berries stared at her bundle and at her sad face. One woman pointed at her. "So, you've lost your Fire? What good does it do you now? Your clan was so selfish and unwilling to share it. Now you're no better off than the rest of us."

The woman laughed a bitter laugh, and the others turned their backs to Thalia. They shunned her, because she had failed.

Slowly, she trudged into the woods again. Her shoulders sagged, her chin rested on her chest.

There were no more tears, so she couldn't cry. There was no more joy, so she couldn't laugh. She was no longer a child, so she couldn't play. And she had let Fire die, so she was no longer the Firetender—she no longer had a purpose. She might as well be dead.

What had happened to the joy she'd known as a child? Before the responsibilities of Fire.

The days drifted by. Thalia kept walking. She heard nothing; she saw nothing; she felt nothing. She could barely eat the berries she found along the way. Weeks passed. Still she kept on, putting one foot in front of the other until she fell to the ground in a sleep of exhaustion.

As she dreamed, an angel, dressed all in white, sat nearby. "Why are you so sad, my child?"

"Because I am a failure. I let Fire die." A tear slipped down Thalia's face.

"Maybe the fire is only sleeping, like you," said the spirit.

"No, no. That can't be true. It is dead and cold."

"The One who began a good work in you will carry it on until it is completed." The angel's voice soothed, like trickling water. For a moment Thalia thought it was Aunt Vesta speaking. But no, her aunt had gone on her final journey.

"I don't understand." She sobbed.

"Our God has made all things from the beginning of time, and He says 'I am the light of the world. Those who follow me will never walk in darkness.' This gift will also be given to you." A warm glow radiated around the angel as she spoke.

"God will give me a gift?" Thalia frowned, puzzled.

"There are different kinds of gifts, and different ways to serve," the angel explained. "Believers share everything they own, including their gifts . . ."

The angel smiled. "God says you are the light of the world … Do not light a lamp and put it under a bowl. Instead, put it on a stand. Then it gives light to everyone …

"Remember …?" The angel's voice was soft. "Remember when you were a child, when you were happy, when you laughed and danced and shared your gift of joy with others? Remember that feeling. It is still there. You are free. Your spirit is alive. There is no one around. Kick up your feet, dance. Try it … try it …" The voice faded.

Slowly, Thalia's eyes opened. The cold from the ground seeped through her. What a strange dream. She could barely remember the joy and the fun she'd had as a young child. There was no way she would ever find that again. No one would ever welcome her, love her, laugh with her again. She had no Fire. Her heart was as cold as the embers. She wanted to just stay there and die, like Fire.

Gradually, the morning sun rose and warmed the earth where she lay. Even though she didn't want to feel or hear anything anymore, the birds calling to each other was music in her ears. She sat up slowly and found herself in a small clearing in the woods. A breeze rustled the leaves, buttercups winked at her from their bed of grass and beckoned with their bright heads. She breathed deeply of the sweet, fresh air.

Hmmm, maybe the angel was right—no one was around. *Nobody's going to yell at me to come tend Fire. Nobody can see me . . .*

No. Thalia hung her head. She couldn't have fun. She didn't deserve it. She didn't have Fire anymore.

But when she looked around her, for the first time in a long time she saw the brilliance of the blue sky, the sunlight glistening through the treetops, the soft, green carpet of grass. Great warmth spread throughout her body. She reached her hands out for her carrying bundle. Trembling, she brought out the container of coals and held it for a long time.

She had worked so very hard to take care of Fire and the needs of the Clan. She had done everything Aunt Vesta had told her to do. She had given up all the fun things she did as a child to feed Fire. She just couldn't do it all herself. If what the angel said about God was true…

"Maybe I need help…" Thalia looked up into the clear blue sky. "God, if you can hear me, I can't do this by myself. If you made everything, then you made me, and you made Fire. Show me what to do."

Thalia became aware of a warmth in her hands. She stroked the clay pot. Could it be…? She slowly opened it. Was there a chance…? With her heart thudding like the drums on her Celebration Day, Thalia blew softly on the dark coals. She blew again, a little more forcefully.

Wait! Was that a spark? Something stirred in her chest. There it was! An amber glow began softly, and grew until the entire pot was pulsating with light and heat.

"It's not dead. Fire is alive!" She had lost Fire—and herself—when she allowed others' demands to drown her own spark.

A tune came unbidden to her mind, and her toes wriggled in her moccasins. Slowly she slid them off and felt the warm earth on her bare feet. She dug her toes into the grass. Her right heel began rocking up and down with the rhythm in her head. As her mouth opened, the tune came rolling out. Before she could think to stop herself, she was singing and dancing through the field of yellow. She stooped to gather flowers to her face, breathed in their perfume, let the soft petals slip through her fingers. A laugh bubbled up and burst through her lips. Tears rolled down her face.

As Thalia danced to the edge of the clearing, tingles rose on the back of her neck. She stopped and looked up. During her dark journey, she had wandered in a circle. The women of the last clan who had shunned her were watching, their mouths open in amazement.

"I have found Fire again! God gave my gift back." She danced up and down. "Let me show you. I will teach you how to keep Fire, to feed it and to bank it carefully at night. I want to share it with you so that you can keep warm and cook your food. Fire was God's gift, and it did not belong to my clan alone. It feels so good to have Fire again!"

Thalia laughed and skipped around the astonished women. She placed a glowing coal onto a pile of twigs and fanned it. The clan gathered in a circle around her and Fire as the flames took hold of the branches and began to dance.

Thalia went from clan to clan, sharing her Fire with everyone. The clanspeople, remembering her great artistic gift with beadwork, gave her beads, sinews and bone needles in an exchange of gratitude. Her stash of coals never dwindled, but instead grew. From deep inside joy bubbled, and she experienced a light-heartedness she'd not had for such a long time. She smiled and laughed again as she shared her gift and the message from God with others: "All things are possible when you give Him your burden and ask for help."

+++

The last clan she would visit was her own. The night before she left for home, she lay down on a pile of furs under the starry sky, thinking about her family. Would they welcome her back—now that she had Fire again? Perhaps she was a permanent outcast, especially since she had shared the gift with other clans. Fear buzzed inside like a disturbed bee hive.

Finally she drifted into a restless sleep. The voice of the angel spoke. "You are a brave young woman. You have lived through the cold and darkness. By accepting God's gift and sharing it with others, you found yourself. With God, all things are possible."

Peace surrounded Thalia like a warm blanket.

The next morning, she set off for her home, breath held, shoulders tight around her ears, and legs wobbly. As she entered the clearing, one of the elder mothers looked up and gave a cry. "Thalia! You've come home!" She rushed forward and enveloped Thalia in a giant hug. Others gathered around and welcomed her in similar fashion.

Thalia released her breath and relaxed her tense shoulders.

The first woman smiled. "At first, we were so angry with you, because you lost Fire. But we were wrong, my dear. We put too much responsibility on your young shoulders, and we were selfish in not sharing Fire. Welcome home."

Each member of the Clan, from the youngest to the oldest, gave her a small gift—just like her Celebration Day. The elder spoke again. "You must take the time to do your beautiful beadwork and to play with the other children. We will help you tend Fire. We realized what we lost when it—and you—were gone. We lost Fire because we were selfish. If we had shared, we wouldn't have had to suffer. Now we know it will not disappear, for others have it as well. Come, let us dance and celebrate."

Thalia smiled and her feet moved to the beat of the music. She had rediscovered *her* Fire.

*Vesta—the Roman goddess of the hearth.
Thalia—Greek, meaning "to Blossom."

THE PIT OF DARKNESS

"Ninety-nine, one hundred…" Glory paused a moment on the steep, rough-hewn stairs that groaned from years of use, and adjusted the heavy basket of coal on her back.

"Climb, girl," boomed a loud voice above her. She began again. "One hundred one, one hundred two…"As she counted, she watched the procession ahead of her. Old women who stooped permanently from their loads, younger women already showing the strain of carrying the baskets of coal up the stairway day after day, year after year, and young girls, like Glory, just beginning their servitude to the land baron who owned the coal mine.

With every birth in the village, parents were forced to sign papers decreeing the child property of the baron. On the day of their 10th birthday, each began work in the mine, the boys digging and loading the baskets alongside their fathers, and the girls carrying the coal to the surface, one basket load at a time. The meager schooling and their freedom stopped on this day.

Today was Glory's first day in the mine—her 10th birthday. Already, her back ached and her feet were like the lumps of coal she carried. The vague memory of a motherly woman reciting a bit of verse flitted through her mind, "Give up your burden, all ye who are weary…"

Oh, if only someone *would* take their burden… But here, where they came to work at dusk and worked through the long night, was nothing but darkness and heavy loads. No, the one who said that surely had never come down here.

"One hundred forty-nine, one hundred fifty." She counted aloud.

Someone groaned in the darkness. "Must you remind us how many steps we have to endure all night long?"

"We should look at the bright side," chirped Glory. "Counting the steps and multiplying them by the number of trips gives us practice at numbers and keeps our minds off how much our feet and backs hurt."

"Well, that'll soon get old." Another voice growled directly behind her. "Pretty soon you'll want only to forget it all."

They became silent as they reached the top, slipped the straps from their shoulders, and tipped the baskets into the waiting wagon. Turning to head back down the stairway, Glory looked at the person behind her. She was surprised to see a teen-aged girl, her hair matted with coal dust and sweat, her shoulders already rounded, and her voice tired and defeated.

Glory sprang down the steps. Oh, no. That wouldn't happen to her. She was going to get out of here soon. She felt it in her heart.

For she knew that she did not belong here. She was taller than the others, and her light blond hair and fair skin contrasted with the swarthiness of everyone else. Her coal miner parents told her that they had found her as a baby, lying in an exquisitely-made basket along the path as they trudged home from the mine.

"You were dressed all in lace and looked like royalty," her mother said. "But no one has ever come to claim you." They had quickly adopted her as their own and signed her over to the baron. For each additional child, he allowed parents more points to buy food from his storehouse. And so Glory became an indentured servant in the baron's mine, along with her parents, brothers and sisters.

But the very nature that kept her looking for the bright side of every dark cloud made her believe her real parents were looking for her. Someday soon they would come to rescue her. She had an oh-so-very faint memory of light and happiness. So, down into the pit she went to get her next loaded basket.

She would become used to this, she promised herself. She would get stronger as the days went by. And she did. Her muscles hardened, and she kept her emotions cheerful.

Even though the others laughed at her optimism and grumbled about her enthusiasm, she sang songs to take her mind off the pain in her back, and made up games in her head to ease the sting of the raw blisters on her feet.

Maybe she really was a princess, and all the king's men were scouring the forests in search of her. They must know about this mine. Surely they would be here any day.

But the weeks and the months went by, and it became harder to think happy thoughts, harder to smile and sing. Her back, legs, and feet ached constantly. The other workers' grumbling and harsh oaths tore at her good mood and her heart grew sad and heavy. The darkness seemed to close around her more and more. The lanterns that lit the passageway seemed to dim. Since she was required to work at night and spent her days nestled in her small, dark sleeping chamber, she seldom saw the sun. Exhausted, she immediately fell into a fitful sleep each morning, chased in her dreams by dark shadows with gnashing teeth and long sharp claws. She began to think of ways to escape her servitude.

One night the guard posted by the lorries stepped into the woods and was not looking her direction. Her heart pounded. She quickly slipped the load, basket and all, into the wagon and ran down the path, away from the mouth of the pit.

"Halt." The guard returned in time to see her run. "Escape," he shouted, striking a huge gong near the wagons. Instantly, a small army of guards took off running after Glory. She ducked into the woods and leaped over dead logs, running for her life. The thought of freedom spurred her on, and she began to outdistance her pursuers.

I'm going to make it. She ran with great hope in her heart. Then a huge branch smacked her in the forehead. Dazed, she fell to the ground, weeping, until the baron's guards caught up to her and carried her back to the mine.

They tied her to another woman whom they threatened with death if Glory tried to escape again. After that, Glory could no longer sing songs and play games to keep her mind off her plight. She simply placed one foot in front of the other through the endless nights. Soon she too began to grumble about the heartlessness of the evil Baron. He, who sat in his mansion on the hill, drinking wine, eating fine meals, and entertaining beautiful maidens. Glory resented the guards who never let the women stop to rest more than a few seconds at a time, who yelled at them to hurry, walk faster, and carry bigger loads. It became harder for her adopted mother to wake her each evening to go to work, and she often skipped the bath that helped soothe her aching muscles and kept her reasonably clean. Her fair hair became dark and matted with coal dust.

Hopelessness engulfed her. No one would come for her. She would be there until she died.

The woman she was tethered to tried to encourage her at first, but soon gave up as Glory sullenly refused to talk. The woman—she didn't care to know her name—was behind her every step, watching her, pushing her, simply another part of her burden. Once, when the woman stumbled and nearly fell, Glory lashed out at her. "Watch where you're going. You nearly pulled me down!"

The others no longer smiled at her. The guards merely shouted, "Hey you, keep moving!" The other women kept their heads down to avoid her hateful stares or sharp words. The woman tied to her begged the guards to be released. There was no more light in Glory. All was darkness inside her.

When she slept, dark creatures tormented her dreams. She would awaken, sweating and shivering with fear. But sometimes a soft, gentle voice would enter her dreams between dragons' battles and the screams of lost souls.

"I am the light of the World. Those who follow me will never walk in darkness. They will have the light that leads to life." A dim memory came to her of soft arms and mother's milk and a soothing voice singing, "Jesus loves me, this I know..."

Glory shook it off. No, it can't be. *I was only a baby. I wouldn't be able to remember such things.*

One night when she came to work she was tied to a different woman. She couldn't help but stare, for this one was not like the other women in the mine. She appeared to be older and yet she did not stoop under her basket. A warm glow surrounded her, her hair was fair and clean, and her face shone with her smile.

"Hello, Glory, I am Angelica, your new partner. Together we will carry the load and keep each other company as we work." She hummed as they set off to climb the steps, much the way Glory had once done.

She only grunted at this woman's words, not wanting to be cheered up. What was the use? She just wanted to forget all this. There was no way out. There was no use trying to take her mind off it.

But Angelica reached back and gently took Glory's hand. Suddenly the stairs didn't seem quite so steep. The older woman sang, "Jesus loves me, this I know..." Glory listened to the sweet, clear voice with awe, and without realizing it, she saw that they were at the top already, to dump their baskets.

All night, the two flew up and down the stairs, or so it seemed to Glory. Angelica sang songs and told her stories about someone named God, who loved Glory and had sent his only son to die on a cross so that Glory would be free. Those little bits of memory stirred inside her head. She had heard something about this before...

"But if He did all that, why am I still here tied to you, and a slave to the mine baron?"

"You must believe with all your heart," Angelica replied. "You must take your darkness and your sadness and your heavy, heavy load and give it to God."

"But where is this God? How can I give this to him if I can't see him?"

"He is already in your heart. He can see that you are in pain, and He wants to take it away. Talk to Him and ask Him for help," the woman explained.

That morning, instead of falling asleep immediately, Glory lay awake thinking of what Angelica had said. She felt a little silly with the thought of talking to someone she couldn't see. But, what if this God person was really listening? What if He really could help? There was no other way out of the pit. She had tried to believe her real parents would come to rescue her. She had tried to escape, both in her mind and by running away. Nothing had worked.

Tears trickled down her cheeks. "Ah… h-hello… God," she stammered. "If you really are here and can hear me—I could use some help. I am living in darkness and cannot escape. I know I don't belong here, but I don't know where to go or how to get there. I must believe in you, for I can no longer believe in anything else." Glory heard no one answer. She was sobbing now. Was it still hopeless? She couldn't merely give up.

That night when she reached the bottom of the mine pit, she was not tied to anyone. She couldn't see Angelica anywhere. So she accepted the heavy basket and turned toward the stairs. As she raised her foot to climb, she glanced off to the side and saw an opening in the stone wall.

In the light stood Angelica, beckoning. Glory glanced quickly around. No one seemed to be watching, so she ducked through the door.

"Follow me." Angelica led her through a brightly lit tunnel. They climbed gradually upward and soon reached another door.

Angelica stopped and turned. "God sent me to rescue you, because you believed in his message." She smiled. "He has said, 'Let light shine out of darkness.' Through that door is a new life for you. God has taken your burden, and brought you out of darkness into his wonderful light. Go and sing his praises to all that you meet." The door opened, and she was gone.

Glory stepped outside. The sun shone brightly through the trees, birds sang, crickets chirped and warm breezes sighed. She felt warm and light, as though the wind could blow her away.

Through a clearing ahead, Glory saw an army of soldiers on horseback riding toward her. Leading the throng, under a flag embroidered with a large cross, were a King and Queen, both dressed in white.

Glory gasped. She hadn't simply imagined another life after all. Suddenly her knees turned to water and she sank to the ground.

The Queen galloped up to her amidst great cheering and slid from her horse. A tall woman with flowing blond hair and a mirror image of Glory, she knelt beside her. "Our long-lost daughter!" she cried. "You were stolen, and we've been searching for so long, but we were thwarted by the force of evil." Tears flowed from her sea-blue eyes.

Glory gazed up at her, bewildered and overcome with relief. A queen. Her mother was a queen. She wouldn't have to work in the pit any longer. Hugging the Queen, she allowed her tears to mingle with the older woman's. Then she pulled away. "What about all the others?"

The Queen gestured toward the evil baron, bound up like a mummy and tied to a horse.

The handsome King declared in a booming voice, "We have captured the force of evil and sent forth the prisoners from the waterless pit."

Glory nodded. "What about my parents who adopted me?"

"They will be well-taken care of. They can come and live with us all in the castle." The Queen reached out and touched Glory's hair. "I am so happy. God led us to you. We have found you at last."

Glory could smile again. She had come home.

THE MAGIC CLOAK

Once upon a time a boy named Nicholas lived with his parents in a tiny cottage in the deep woods. His father was a poor woodcutter who worked hard every day to supply firewood to the townsfolk. His mother was a simple woman, who kept a tidy home and stirred up delicious soup from whatever she had available.

Nicholas was extremely shy. He never, ever went into town, and they rarely had visitors at their rough-hewn little hut. When a village dweller out for a stroll or a hunter stopped by, Nicholas would run and hide. Because he was small for his age, he became quite good at hiding in wee spaces.

His mother usually offered the visitor some soup. Sometimes the guest would sit a spell to eat and to tell his mother all the latest news from town.

When they had company, Nicholas would peek out from his hiding place—under the bed, behind the door or inside the clothes closet. His mother would try to coax him to come out and talk to them. But strangers asked a lot of silly questions, like "How old are you?" or "Do you like living way out here in the woods?"

Nicholas shrank back into the darkness of his hiding place and stayed there until long after the visitor had gone.

Then one day when Nicholas hid in the musty trunk under the stairs, he found an old black cloak. He put it on and immediately felt safe and warm. He pulled the hood up over his head and climbed out of the trunk to show his mother what he had found. As he walked into the kitchen, he stopped short, for a visitor was still there. Nicholas held his breath and got ready to run away.

But the stranger looked right past him and continued to talk to his mother. Even she paid no attention to Nicholas.

What had just happened? Why had they acted like he wasn't even there? He went into the forest to think about this.

Nicholas liked to go into the woods to play. He never saw anyone but his friends—brown furry squirrels, gray field mice, and colorful feathered songbirds. Sometimes, if he sat quite still, a fawn would come near, almost close enough to touch his outstretched hand. Nicholas loved the animals, and they never seemed frightened of him.

As he sat, his black cloak around him, thinking of his quiet life in the woods, he was startled by a noise. Like the rabbit that nibbled near his toes, he froze. A large man walked by with a deer slung over his back. Nicholas shook with fear. He was sure the hunter would hear his heart beating, it echoed so loudly in his head. But even though the man walked within just a few feet of Nicholas, he seemed to look straight through him.

After a long time, Nicholas uncoiled his nearly-paralyzed legs and slowly stood to go home. He thought about the hunter and wondered why this sharp-eyed tracker had not noticed him.

+++

As the days went by, Nicholas wandered farther and farther from his home, always wearing his black cloak. Sometimes he sat for hours watching a pair of black bear cubs play near their den. The mother bear sunned herself nearby, but never bothered Nicholas.

One afternoon, he discovered the cave where an old hermit lived. Nicholas had heard stories about him from his father—how he yelled and chased after anyone who came near. Nicholas saw the smoke from the old man's fire and smelled meat cooking. His stomach growled. He had been away from home all day with nothing to eat. But he didn't want the man to see him and yell at him or chase him. The hermit sat at the mouth of his cave, nodding in the sun. With slow, quiet steps, Nicholas crept toward the fire. The man never moved. Closer and closer, Nicholas came.

A twig snapped under his foot, and Nicholas froze like a frightened rabbit. The hermit started, and looked around. But he merely grunted and drifted off to sleep again. Nicholas couldn't believe it. He walked slowly to the fire, took out his knife and cut off a hunk of roasting meat. Then he ran behind a tree, squatted and ate, savoring the rich flavor. Every once in a while the old man would awaken and look toward him, but nothing happened.

Nicholas was still hungry, so he crept back to the fire for another piece of meat. He scrunched his forehead. The man must be blind. He finished eating and retreated into the woods, still watching the hermit. By and by, the man got up and walked to the fire to turn the meat on the spit. Then he picked up a book and began to read. Nicholas shook his head. Hmm, how strange.

He turned and ran home as if a fire were chasing his tail. He wondered about the hermit. And what about the visitors who had paid him no mind? Even his parents ignored him when he wore the warm black cloak. This cloak must be magic. He could go anywhere he wanted to, and he would never have to talk to anyone or answer any silly questions, ever again.

After that, he wore the safe black cloak every day, except when he wanted to sit down to eat with his father and mother, or to listen to them read, or tell stories by the fire in the evening before he went to bed.

Nicholas became braver and wandered farther from home every day. Sometimes he stopped by the unsuspecting hermit's fire and stole a bit of food again. He laughed to himself, wondering what the old man thought about his missing meat. He probably believed it was a wild animal.

The carefree days passed, and Nicholas roamed and dreamed his way through the forest, making up stories in his head about dragons and dragon slayers who wore black cloaks and looked very much like Nicholas.

One morning, he was walking and dreaming and dreaming and walking. Suddenly he shook himself, as though he were just waking up from a nap. Nicholas found himself at the edge of a town. Oh no! He was lost. He had no idea how he had gotten here. His mouth was dry and his palms wet.

But wait. All he had to do was turn around and go back the way he had come. Nicholas turned to cross the meadow and go back to his beloved woods. He walked and he walked, and he walked some more. The sun rose higher in the sky, and Nicholas became very hungry and thirsty. He looked behind him at the town, and it seemed as close as when he had started. And the forest seemed as far away.

Nicholas sat down to rest. What was he to do? Well, he had his magical cloak on, didn't he? He might as well go back into the town and see if he could find something to eat and drink. Nobody was likely to pay any attention to him.

So he turned and walked toward the town. Pretty soon he came to a large building, where he could smell wonderful cooking aromas. He followed the sound of laughter and music and walked around the building, looking for an entrance. But all the doors he found were locked.

Curious, he went to a window and peeked in. He saw a large group of people inside, singing and laughing, playing music and dancing, eating and drinking. Nicholas tried to open the window, but it, too, was stuck. Oh well, he'd simply have to go find another house where something was cooking. He walked on. Soon he came to a hut, but the door there was locked, too, and he couldn't smell anything cooking. Probably nobody was home anyway.

Nicholas went to the next house, and the next. It was the same everywhere. He couldn't get in, even when he could see someone inside.

By this time, it was getting dark, and his stomach was growling as loud as a big mother bear protecting her cubs. He shivered in the cold. He'd better start for home again. His mother and father would be worried about him if he wasn't back for supper.

Nicholas walked and walked. Again, the more he walked, the farther away the forest seemed. The night grew colder and darker. Weak with hunger, he sank to his knees in the meadow, then curled up on his side, and pulled the cloak tight around him. He was lost. He couldn't find his way back home.

Hot tears spilled down his cheeks as he pictured his parents sitting in front of the fire, eating hot soup. A dark, cold panic rumbled up inside him, and he wondered if he would die. Suddenly his fear of people seemed very small compared to this new anxiety that grew stronger by the minute.

He sobbed. "What am I going to do?" Then a thought came to him. He could just take off the cloak and go ask someone in the village for food and to show him the way home. Yes, that is what he would do. Surely in one of these houses must be a nice woman, like his mother, who would feed him something warm.

Nicholas ran back to the town. When he came to the first house where he smelled food, he whipped back the folds of the cloak to take it off. But it would not come off! Nicholas searched for the front opening, but he couldn't find it. Maybe it had gotten turned around on his body. He twisted the back to the front and tried again. It still would not come off. He tried to shove the hood back from his head, but it would not move either.

What was happening? Was he doomed to wear this cloak forever? If he wore the cloak, no one would ever see him again. And no one would know that he was hungry and tired and lost and so lonely. Nicholas sank to the ground, crying again. He would die.

Why had he ever been so afraid of people? Why had he found this stupid cloak? It wasn't so wonderful, after all. Now he was invisible forever, and no one would even know he existed.

"Oh, help me. Someone please help me!" He sobbed and sobbed.

After a while Nicholas became aware of a light nearby. He looked up and blinked. Then he rubbed his fists into his eyes. A figure stood at the edge of the woods. It wore flowing white garments and was bathed in a warm glow. Was he dead already?

The figure beckoned to him.

Nicholas stood with shaking knees. "You can see me?"

"Follow me." The figure beckoned again.

Nicholas walked toward the light. "Who are you? How can you see me?"

The figure of light walked into the forest, turning to crook a finger at Nicholas. "Follow me," he said again.

Nicholas followed the light through the darkness, wondering if he were dreaming. "Who… who are you?"

"I am the light of the world. Those who follow me will never walk in darkness. They will have the light that leads to life."

"Huh?" Why was this person talking in riddles? And where was he leading Nicholas? But he was curious. The warmth and light comforted and drew him onward. They walked on through the woods, and soon Nicholas recognized where he was. He was getting closer to home. The person reached out and took his hand.

"The Lord, your God, will hold your right hand … Fear not, I will help you."

"Why are you helping me?"

The figure stopped in a clearing near Nicholas' house. "Because I love you. I am the way and the truth and the life." He placed a hand on Nicholas' shoulder. Nicholas grew warmer and the cloak gently fell away.

"You won't be needing this anymore. God is your refuge and strength, a real help when you are in trouble. He is who you've been looking for. He is your help and your shield."

Nicholas stared in awe.

"Be strong and have courage, do not be afraid, for the Lord is with you wherever you go."

Nicholas watched the light fade slowly away, leaving a glowing mist behind as the rising sun warmed the sky. He stood outside his house, wondering what had just happened.

The front door opened, and his mother stepped out, giving a sharp little cry when she saw him. "Nicholas, you're back!" Her voice choked in a sob, and she drew him to her in a warm hug. "Oh, I'm so glad. Are you all right?"

Nicholas nestled in her comforting arms. "Yes, Mama, I'm just fine."

"We were so worried. I couldn't sleep for the longest time. But then I had the strangest dream. I saw you walking through the woods toward home, and an angel was guiding you!"

Nicholas' eyes grew big and round. "Th…that's exactly what happened! I got lost and went to a village and nobody could see me and I was so hungry and so thirsty and so cold and so tired and scared and I thought I was already dead…" His voice trailed off.

"You know, sweetheart, we have a book that I have not read for a very long time." His mother's voice was soft. "Come inside. I will fix you a warm breakfast, and I will read to you. I think this book will explain what happened."

They went inside, where Nicholas' father gave him a great bear hug, and fed him warm oatmeal. Then his mother read to him from the Holy Bible:

"My help comes from the Lord who made heaven and earth …The Lord will preserve you from all evil; he will preserve your soul. The Lord will preserve your going out and your coming in from this time forth, and even forevermore." *Psalm 121.*

Nicholas curled closer to his mother and father next to the fire and smiled, his heart filled with love. He need never be afraid again.

THE END

AUTHOR AFTERWORD

A man, traveling across the desert with his wagon and oxen, came upon another man walking. In the heat of the day, there was no shade for miles, and the poor man staggered beneath the weight of a large, heavy sack he carried over his shoulder.

"Come, my good fellow, climb aboard. I'll give you a ride," said the man in the wagon.

"Oh no, I must continue. I have this load to deliver." The fellow on foot kept walking.

The first man blinked his eyes and shook his head in puzzlement. "But it's terribly hot, and you have such a heavy load. I'm headed your direction, anyway. Why not just hop in and ride?"

The second man continued walking, resolutely putting one foot in front of the other. "No, no. I can't."

The wagon owner insisted, following alongside. "Just get in, you can ride in the back."

Finally, the weary foot traveler stopped. "All right." He climbed up on the wagon.

"Well, good. It only makes sense." The first man gee-upped his oxen forward, and they continued down the sandy trail. As they traveled, the wagon driver thought his passenger might be thirsty, so he reached down, grabbed his waterskin and turned to offer it. His arm stopped in mid-air. He was at a loss for words.

There the man stood, in the back of the wagon, still clutching the heavy sack over his shoulder.

+++

I heard this story at a women's retreat several years ago. It was at a time when I faced some difficult decisions about my job. I had always known about the verse from the Bible that tells us to "give up your burden," but somehow in the desperation of my situation, I had forgotten it. I was like the man with the sack, refusing any help, stubbornly holding onto my load, trying to carry it all myself—when I didn't need to!

Looking back, I can see that as soon as I made the decision to "give up my burden," doors began closing and opening, and my path became clear to me. It became possible for me to make the decision to retire from that job and return to my lifelong love—writing.

Each of the stories in this book is about "giving up your burden"—the burden of fear and mistrust, the burden of too much responsibility and perfectionism, the burden of darkness and adversity, and the burden of shyness and fear.

No matter what kind of problem you may be facing, remember Matthew 11:28, *"Come to me, all you who are tired and carrying heavy loads. I will give you rest."*

+++

Thank you to all the critique groups (starting in Missoula, MT when I wrote the first story; Mount Vernon and Bellingham, WA; and in Chino Valley and Prescott Valley, AZ) who have helped me over the years to hone my craft and make my stories better. Thank you to my beta readers for this book: Natalie Bright, Brenda Cox Clayton, Barbara Jaquay (who was also instrumental in helping craft the Q&A for the book), Milan Marsenich, and Mary Trimble. I couldn't have done it without all of you, and of course, God's help and inspiration.

Heidi M. Thomas

Questions for Discussion

If you as a parent or a teacher would like to use this book for discussion, here are some possible questions. For help with answers, visit www.heidimthomas.com

SECRET OF THE ICE CASTLE

1. What does the waterfall represent?
2. Why do you think they wouldn't let her go out into the world?
3. What do the princess' trips into the world represent?
4. What does the locket stand for?

THE FIRETENDER

1. What is represented by the child's happiness and willingness to accept the responsibility of being an adult?
2. What does the heavy burden of maintaining the fire mean?
3. What do the different clans personify?

THE PIT OF DARKNESS

1. What is the significance of hauling coal up the stairs, day after day?
2. Who does Angelica represent?
3. What does finding her family mean?

THE MAGIC CLOAK

1. What does the cloak represent?
2. Not being able to find his way home exemplifies what?
3. What does being unable to remove the cloak mean?

AUTHOR AFTERWORD

1. Why don't we turn our burdens over to God?
2. What keeps us from surrendering to Him?

About the Author

Heidi M. Thomas grew up on a working ranch in eastern Montana, riding and gathering cattle for branding and shipping. Her parents taught her a love of books, and her grandmother rode bucking stock in rodeos. She followed her dream of writing, with a journalism degree from the University of Montana. Heidi is the author of the award-winning (adult and YA-suitable) "Cowgirl Dreams" novel series, based on her grandmother, and *Cowgirl Up: A History of Rodeo Women*. Novels *Seeking the American Dream* and *Finding True Home* are based on her mother who emigrated from Germany after WWII. She makes her home in North-Central Arizona. www.heidimthomas.com

About the Illustrator

Susie Talbot, wife for 53 years, mother of three grown children and seven grandchildren, has pursued a myriad of art genres over the years. Presently, she's enjoying ink-to-paper drawing  Zentangles on 4 x 4-inch "tiles," and painting rocks or doing crafts with her grandchildren. Before digital photography, she worked as a photographic retouch artist for professional photo labs for about seven years in the States and when she and her family lived in Australia. To Susie, it's all about enjoying the process and about giving God the glory in it all.

www.ingramcontent.com/pod-product-compliance
Lightning Source LLC
Chambersburg PA
CBHW042013120726
47911CB00029B/916